The Andalite's Gift

PART I

Look for other ANIMORPHS™
titles by K.A. Applegate:

ANIMORPHS

<MEGAMORPHS #1>

The Andalite's Gift PART I

K.A. Applegate

AN
APPLE
PAPERBACK

SCHOLASTIC INC.
New York Toronto London Auckland Sydney

Cover illustration by David B. Mattingly

ISBN 0-590-29842-9

12 11 10 9 8 7 6 5 4 3 2 1   7 8 9/9 0 1 2/0

Printed in the U.S.A.   40

First Scholastic printing, June 1997

For Jean Feiwel, Craig Walker, and
Tonya Alicia Martin,
who morph my scribbles into books.

And, as always, for Michael

The Andalite's Gift

PART I

CHAPTER 1

Jake

My name is Jake. Just Jake. No last name. Or at least no last name I can tell you.

I am an Animorph. I guess that makes me one of the most hunted, endangered species on Earth. The Yeerks want me dead. They want my friends dead. So if they knew who I was, and how to find me, I wouldn't have a chance.

That's why I won't tell you my last name. And I won't tell you what city or state I live in. Because I want to go on living. I want to go on living so I can go on fighting *them*.

Are you one of those people who looks up at the night sky and wonders whether there is life out there among the stars? Do you wonder about

UFO's? Do you wonder whether aliens will ever come to Earth?

Well, stop wondering. The Yeerks are here.

They're a species of parasites — just little slugs, really. Little slugs that crawl inside your head and wrap themselves around your brain and make you do whatever they want you to do.

When that happens you stop being a true human being. You become a Controller. That's what we call a human who is under the control of a Yeerk. When you talk to a Controller, you may be looking at a human face, you may hear a human voice, but what you're really talking to is a Yeerk.

And they are everywhere. If you think you haven't seen one, you're wrong. The policeman in his patrol car, the clerk at the grocery store, your teacher, your pastor, your doctor: Any of them might be a Controller. Your mother, father, sister, or best friend: They could all be Controllers.

I know. My brother Tom is one of them. They have taken my brother from me and made him an enemy. I sit at the breakfast table every morning and make small talk, knowing all the while that Tom is not Tom anymore.

And they have taken my best friend's mother. Everyone thinks Marco's mother is dead. Only he and I know the truth: She, too, is one of *them*.

They are everywhere. They can be anyone.

They tear lives apart. They do unspeakable things. And we stand against them alone. Only we know the threat. We six: five Animorphs and one Andalite.

Five human kids with the power to become any animal we can touch. And a kid from another planet who looks like some weird mix of deer, human, and scorpion.

The six of us against all the might of the Yeerks, and all the evil genius of their leader, Visser Three.

Which is why Rachel was worried about leaving, even for a weekend.

We were all together that Friday evening — Marco, Cassie, Tobias, Rachel, and me. Ax wasn't there because he would have had to change into his human morph. He doesn't like to become human. I think he feels naked without his deadly tail.

So it was just the five of us in Cassie's barn, surrounded by all the chattering, snuffling, chirping, preening (and smelly) animals in their cages. The barn is also the Wildlife Rehabilitation Center. Cassie's parents are veterinarians. They use their barn to take in sick or injured wild animals.

"It's just this stupid, two-day gymnastics camp I signed up for a long time ago," Rachel was saying. "It's no big deal. It's something I was going to do back . . . you know, *before*."

"Rachel, you should go," Cassie said. "Our entire lives cannot be about fighting the Yeerks. We have to try to be seminormal. I mean, it can't all be danger and battle and fear, right? So go. But for now, help me lift up this crow's cage. He's going up on that shelf."

Cassie was trying to get us to help clean up the barn. We used the barn to get together. It was one of the few places we could meet with Tobias. See, he can't exactly go to the mall.

<Crows,> Tobias said, in thought-speak that we heard only in our minds. <I can't believe you're saving a crow. I hate crows. You know how he probably got that broken wing? Trying to mob a respectable hawk, that's how. Crows are total punks.>

Tobias was perched high in the rafters of the barn. From up there he could fly in and out through the hayloft. Tobias is a red-tailed hawk. Actually, in his mind, in his soul, he's human. But the power to morph has a terrifying downside. Stay in morph for more than two hours, and you stay forever. Tobias was trapped forever in a body with long, powerful wings, ripping, taloned feet, and fierce, angry eyes that stared at you around his hooked beak.

You would never guess that he had once been such a gentle guy. I guess he still is that guy. But he's also a hawk.

4

<Yeah, I'm looking at *you*, crow,> Tobias said in mock threat. Obviously, the crow did not understand thought-speak.

Cassie smiled. "Tobias, I promise when we release this guy, we'll take him far from your territory."

"I already told Melissa Chapman I wasn't going," Rachel said, going back to her own topic. "She went up to the camp this afternoon, right after school."

Marco, who had been lying back on a big bale of hay and staring at the ceiling, sat up. "Rachel doesn't think we can survive without her for two days. After all, she's the mighty *Xena: Warrior Princess*."

It was Marco's teasing name for Rachel. Rachel has a tendency to be very bold. Anytime there's something borderline-insane that needs to be done, Rachel is always the first volunteer.

"Marco? You have hay stuck in your hair," Rachel said.

He ignored her remark. "Rachel thinks if she's not here and we have trouble, we'll all just run screaming and yammering like a bunch of scared little kids." He put on a phony-serious expression. "All I want to know is this: Why don't you dress like Xena? I mean, the whole leather and sword thing would really work for you."

"Okay, shut up, I'll go," Rachel said. "I'll go.

I'm going. Just to get away from Marco for a couple days. I'll catch the bus tomorrow morning."

"Think of me when you're on the uneven parallel bars," Marco said.

But it wasn't to Marco that Rachel looked. It was to Tobias. "You guys *will* stay out of trouble while I'm gone, won't you?"

<We'll be fine, Rachel,> Tobias said.

I saw Cassie smile, and my gaze met hers. She gave a slight nod. Cassie has a theory that Rachel and Tobias like each other. Not that Rachel has ever said anything, even though Rachel and Cassie are best friends. Cassie thinks it's sweet and romantic. I just think it's kind of sad. I mean, as far as we know, Tobias will never be fully human again.

"We should all just enjoy a nice, normal weekend," I said. "Have normal fun. We've had plenty of danger and excitement."

Marco sent me a sly, resentful look. "*Some* of us are going to have more fun than some others. *Some* of us are going to pool parties that *some* of us were not invited to." He shook his fists melodramatically at the ceiling. "Why? Why? What does that girl have against me?"

I rolled my eyes. "Here we go again."

Cassie rescued me. "I need someone strong to come outside with me, help me carry in some new cages from the truck. Marco?"

"Oh! My back!" Marco cried. "A sudden, shooting pain."

"I'm coming, Cassie," I said. I gave Marco a shove, pushing him back on his bale of hay. "You are so pathetic."

"Don't strain yourself," Marco said with a cocky grin.

Outside, out of the golden glow of the barn's lights, it was getting dark. A full moon had risen, and you could just see the first stars off to the east.

The pickup truck was piled precariously high with wire cages. I climbed up and began to untie the rope that held them in place.

"It seems strange — Rachel going away — even for a couple days," Cassie said. "And it seems even stranger that it would seem strange. I mean, it should be no big deal."

"Well, I guess when life turns completely crazy, it's the normal things that start to seem strange."

Cassie nodded slowly. For a while she said nothing. She just stood there with her arms crossed, looking up at the moon.

I climbed down off the truck. "What's bothering you?"

She shrugged. "Nothing. Just . . . a feeling. I don't know. Bad dreams, I guess."

"I have those, too," I said. "We all do. You

can't live through all this and not have it bother you. What's the dream about? The ant thing?"

We'd morphed ants once. We'd gone down into an ant tunnel and had been attacked by an enemy colony of ants. No one wanted to go through that, ever again. Not ever.

"No, not the ants," Cassie said. "At least not directly. It's . . . it's dumb. There's . . . something. I don't even know what it is. But it's not a good thing. And it asks me to make a choice. In the dream I have to decide who lives and who dies."

I moved closer to Cassie and put my arm around her shoulder. There were goose bumps on her bare arms.

"I never used to be afraid, Jake," Cassie said. "Not of anything. And now it's like I'm afraid all the time."

"You deal with it, though," I said. It made me nervous talking about feelings like this. I guess I think if you just don't talk about the fear, it will go away. "You always deal with it," I repeated.

"So far," Cassie said softly. "So far."

8

CHAPTER 2
Rachel

My name is Rachel. I live with my mom and my two little sisters. We live pretty close to Jake, who lives pretty close to Marco. Cassie is the farthest one out because she lives on a farm.

I guess we're a pretty average bunch of kids. I mean, we *were* a pretty average bunch. Marco lives with his dad. I live with my mom. Jake and Cassie each have both parents around. We go to school. We do homework. We hang at the mall. We listen to music. Go to movies on the weekend. Normal. Boringly average.

Until one night when we happened to hook up together at the mall and decided to take a shortcut through an abandoned construction site off the highway.

We weren't a "group" back then. Jake was my cousin, but we didn't really see each other, except at school. Cassie was my best friend, and had been for a long time. But Marco was just Jake's friend, not mine. And Tobias was this guy Jake felt sorry for because he came from such a messed-up home and got picked on by bullies.

That's Jake: When he sees some guy getting his head stuffed in a toilet at school, he is absolutely going to stop it. Jake isn't some big tough guy or anything. It's just that when he tells you, in that calm, reasonable voice of his, to stop picking on someone, you stop. You just do.

Jake is sort of the one in charge. It's not something he ever wanted. It just seems natural for him to take over.

Not that Jake is without his own level of stupidity. I mean, he was right there with us, walking through an isolated, abandoned construction site that night. Wasn't the smartest thing we ever did.

But the way it turned out, the real danger that night was not from some mad slasher. The real danger was from a totally unexpected direction.

See, that's where the damaged Andalite spaceship landed. Right there in the construction site. That's where we saw our first alien. That's where we learned about the Yeerk threat. And that's where the Andalite, Prince Elfangor, gave us our power to morph.

It's where Elfangor died, too. We watched it happen. We watched that brave, decent, kind creature be murdered by Visser Three. Murdered for trying to protect the people of Earth.

Anyway. That's when we became a group. It was Marco who came up with a name for what we were. *Animorphs.* Persons who can morph animals.

The Andalite left us the burden of fighting the Yeerks, and gave us that one weapon: the power to morph. Like all weapons, it has dangers even to those who use it for a good cause. Just ask Tobias.

But it is an awesome power. We have done some damage to the Yeerks. And to be honest with you, sometimes the morphing power is just plain fun. Right now, though, my "normal" life was calling.

It was already getting warm by the time I walked over to school the next morning. The bus to the camp was due to come at eleven. I got to school an hour early.

I stopped on the sidewalk in front of the school and checked my watch. The sun was climbing fast, and you could tell it was going to be a really hot day. I smiled. It would be a good day for flying.

I crossed the athletic field and headed for the woods behind the school. I wanted to check in with Tobias before I left. It's no big thing. It's just that I kind of take care of stuff Tobias needs. I bring him books sometimes. You know — things he can't get in the woods.

But Tobias isn't always an easy guy to find. Especially in the morning, when he's likely to be out hunting his breakfast. I knew I would need great eyes and speed to find him and still get back in time to catch the bus.

It's funny how it never even occurred to me that I was in a very dangerous position. See, my mom and my friends all thought I was heading to camp. They wouldn't expect to see me for a couple of days. But the camp people didn't think I was coming. So they wouldn't expect to see me, either.

But none of this occurred to me. After all, what did I have to worry about? Little did I know.

So, I entered the woods, put my outer clothing in my bag, hid it beneath some low-lying bushes, and took a quick look around to make sure I was alone. Then I began to morph.

I focused my mind on one of the many animals whose DNA is part of me.

Every morphing is unique. The changes never happen the same way twice. This time, the first thing to change was my mouth. My lips grew hard and stiff. And when I rolled my eyes downward, I could see my mouth become bright yellow and bulge outward.

As that happened, I began to shrink. The pine needle-covered ground came up toward me as I lost a foot of height within a few seconds. Then another foot.

The strangest thing, though, was my skin. The flesh on my bare arms began to melt like candle wax. It melted and ran together. It formed intricate patterns, like a tattoo of feathers. Suddenly, the painted feather patterns were no longer just designs. Actual feathers began to emerge.

The feathers were dark brown, except for the ones that replaced my blond hair and the skin of my face and neck. Those feathers were all snowy white.

By the time the morph was nearly complete, I only stood about two feet tall. My feet had split open and formed yellow talons, each of which ended in a wicked, hooked claw.

My arms rose up, horizontal. Long feathers sprouted from them, even as my solid, heavy, human bones became hollow and light.

It took just a few minutes for the transformation to be done. I was no longer human. I was a bald eagle.

I turned to face the breeze and opened my wings. They stretched six feet from tip to tip. I felt the wind press against my feathers, stretching my muscles. I flapped several times with great power, and then . . . I was airborne! I drew my talons up snug against my body.

I flapped and rose. I flapped more, and soared above the trees. The top branches reached for me but missed. I flapped still more and caught a good, strong headwind. It was like an invisible wedge that forced me up and up.

Up and up! I rose till I was several hundred feet above the treetops. I could see the school down below. I could see the bus parked in the empty lot. And, being an eagle, I could see a great deal more.

Looking through the eyes of an eagle is like having built-in binoculars. From hundreds of feet in the air I could see field mice just poking their noses out of their holes. I could see ants crawling up the trunks of trees. I could look down through the water of a stream and see the tiny fish feeding there. I could see everything, like no human will ever see.

I turned toward the deeper woods where Tobias lived.

Maybe there is something better than flying free, high above the trees, riding the wind, but I doubt it. It was freedom beyond any dream of freedom. I loved it. For all the pain that has come from the war with the Yeerks, I swear sometimes just being able to fly makes it all worthwhile.

I was close to Tobias's territory when I spotted something interesting below me. It was a deer-like animal, running swiftly through the trees. When I focused my laser-intensity eagle sight, I could see the semihuman torso and face and the deadly scorpion tail.

Ax! Or, Aximili-Esgarrouth-Isthill, to use his complete name. Ax is an Andalite. The only Andalite to survive a terrible space battle with the Yeerks. Prince Elfangor was his brother.

It was fun watching him run. I've never seen anything that can look as delicate and cute one minute — and as dangerous the next — as an Andalite.

I decided to swoop down over Ax and say hi. I spilled a little air from my wings and dropped, thrilled by the feeling of a controlled fall from hundreds of feet up. It's like jumping off a skyscraper, knowing you can survive.

I dropped toward the trees.

I actually had time to notice the nest in a high branch. Just out of the corner of my eye. I had time to think, *Isn't that cute? Baby birds.*

And then they hit me.

SWOOP!

SWOOP!

Faster than me! More agile! Small, dark birds zipped straight at me like they were going to hit. Too many of them!

SWOOP! SWOOP! SWOOP!

I turned a hard left. In a flash I knew what was happening. They thought I was attacking their nest. They were "mobbing" me! Trying to drive me off.

I banked a hard turn. Too fast! I was still going fast from the dive. Too fast! Bank left! Turn!

WHAM!

I barely saw the tree trunk before I hit. Head-first.

Down I fell. Down through branches that tore at me, banged me, slapped me, ripped at my feathers.

I hit the ground hard. I was hurt. I knew I was hurt. Fading out. My mind was swimming. Human thoughts . . . eagle instinct, all swirling, shifting. I was falling down, down a dark well.

Down . . .

Morph out, I told myself. *Rachel . . . MORPH OUT!*

And then I was gone.

CHAPTER 3
Marco

"Look, it's simple," I explained patiently. "There's this party. This *pool* party. And I was not invited. Not only was I not invited, but the girl who's having the party went out of her way to *not* invite me."

By the way, hi, my name is Marco. I'm an Animorph, too. I'm the smart, cute one. No, seriously. Jake is the bossy one, Cassie's the nice one, Rachel is the stupidly brave one, and Tobias is a bird.

I am the cute one. All the girls think so. All except Darlene.

<So you are not wanted at this party. But you want to go, anyway?>

That was Ax speaking. Well, not exactly

"speaking." He's an Andalite, and Andalites don't have mouths. They do "thought-speak." It's like telepathy. We can all do it when we're in a morph. But for Andalites it's their normal language. Ax's real name is Aximili-Esgarrouth-Isthill. Rolls right off the tongue, doesn't it? Now you know why we just call him Ax.

"That's right," I explained to him. "I mean, Jake and Cassie were both invited. Rachel was invited, but she's going to that stupid gymnastics thing. Basically, everyone at school was invited. All I'm saying is, there must be a reason why I was not invited. And I think I know what that reason is: Darlene likes me. There's *no* other possible explanation."

Ax looked puzzled. <Is that common among humans? Do you avoid the ones you like?>

"Not like. *Like.* I like you, Ax. But I don't *like* you. There's like, and then there's like, *like.*"

Ax stared at me with his main eyes. He has four eyes altogether. Two of them are fairly normal. The other two eyes are on these stalklike things that stick out of the top of his head like those little horns a giraffe has. On the end of each stalk, he has an eye, which he can point in any direction. Very weird. But you can't sneak up on the guy, that's for sure.

<I am confused,> Ax said.

"It's okay. You don't need to understand. I just want you to go with me."

<To the party?>

"That's right. We have to go to the party to see what Darlene says about me. She and her cheerleader friends are probably going to talk about me. I want to hear what they say."

<And you want me to go with you?>

"Yeah. You and me. I need someone to watch my back."

<But Prince Jake will be at the party, won't he?>

I rolled my eyes. Ax is convinced Jake is his prince. I guess Andalites are into the whole royalty thing.

"Yes, Jake will be there. But Jake is not going to help me spy on Darlene, is he? Neither will Cassie. Cassie doesn't exactly fit in with the cheerleader crowd. They talk about clothes and guys. Cassie talks about animals and saving the world or whatever."

<Pardon me if I sound skeptical, and please don't be offended,> Ax said, <but I sense that maybe this is a dishonorable idea.>

<You sense right, Ax.>

Tobias. He zipped swiftly overhead and landed on a low branch. He was carrying something in his beak.

19

"Hi, Tobias," I said. "Do you have it?"

<Yes. And do you know how hard it is to fly around with a live, squirming mouse in my beak?>

"Drop it down to me," I said.

<You are a twisted, devious human being, Marco,> Tobias said. <Ax, if you have any sense you won't get involved in this.>

<Tobias, I am suffering. I have small, itching bumps on parts of my body. Marco has agreed to help me, if I will help him. He has a rare medicine that will help.>

<Marco, you're blackmailing Ax with flea powder? Ax, my friend, you just picked up a couple fleas. It's normal in the woods. Don't let Marco jerk you —>

"Just give me the mouse and stop acting like a parent," I interrupted. "I'm not blackmailing anyone. I'll bring Ax the flea powder. Jeez. The suspicion around here."

Tobias dropped the mouse and I caught it with one hand. It squirmed and I almost dropped it. But as I began to "acquire" it, it calmed down.

See, if you want to morph into an animal, you have to acquire it first. You have to make contact. Then you sort of focus on it, concentrate on it. The animal goes into a trance. And meanwhile the animal's DNA is being absorbed.

Don't ask me how it works. It's some weird Andalite biotechnology. I just know it works.

When I was done acquiring the mouse I handed it to Ax. He had to use both hands to hold on. Andalite arms and hands are kind of puny. Of course, they also have four legs, and those are pretty strong. I mean, Ax can haul when he wants to. I'll bet he could do forty miles an hour.

Then there's that tail. The tail is the reason Andalites will never be considered truly "cute." I've seen Ax use his tail on full-grown Hork-Bajir warriors. And fast? Man, you don't even see it move. It's like WHAPP! and all of a sudden a Hork-Bajir only has one arm. I believe Ax could chop down a tree with that tail if he felt like it.

<Marco, you know Jake will roast you alive behind this,> Tobias said. <Morphing for personal reasons?>

"Hey, Jake was invited to the party, all right? *He'll* be soaking up the rays at poolside. *He'll* be having a good time. Meanwhile I, his best friend, was not even invited. Jake is big on justice. I ask you: Is this justice? No. Clearly not."

<Marco, Jake says the last time you were invited to one of Darlene's pool parties you floated a Baby Ruth bar in the pool and told everyone it was . . . you know. Maybe that's why you weren't invited.>

"I was like six years old," I protested. "I didn't know any better. Besides, it was funny."

<Marco, you were not six. You were ten.>

"Whatever. Who remembers this stuff?"

<Darlene does.>

I ignored Tobias. "Are you done acquiring the mouse?" I asked Ax. "If so, give him back to Tobias for lunch."

<I've eaten, thanks,> Tobias said. <But you shouldn't laugh. You want to go play mouse, you better remember something: There are a lot of predators who enjoy eating mice. It's a dangerous world out there.>

"And who would know that better than you, Mr. Predator?"

Tobias laughed. <Even we predators get ours sometimes. I saw a bald eagle get mobbed by a bunch of jays this morning. Slammed into a tree. I guess the eagle was going after their nest.>

"There won't be any eagles at the party," I said. "The bird world is your problem, dude. I have a party to attend."

<Darlene likes him,> Ax said. <But she doesn't *like* him.>

<That's pretty much how everyone feels about Marco,> Tobias said with a laugh.

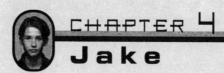

CHAPTER 4
Jake

"I feel bad even going to this party," I said. "Darlene should have invited Marco. He wouldn't have done the Baby Ruth thing again. He's much more mature now. Sort of."

"I feel a little guilty, too," Cassie said. She lowered her voice to a whisper and put her mouth close to my ear. "But I seem to remember you saying we should all take the weekend off and be normal. So I am going to be normal."

We were both in our swim suits, sitting in those long pool chairs. You know — the ones you can adjust so you're lying down or sitting up.

There were forty or fifty kids around the pool. Darlene's family has money, I guess, because it's a very nice pool.

There was a long table loaded up with chips and dip and cold cuts. And there were coolers full of iced soft drinks. There was decent rock music playing on the stereo. Some kids were dancing.

It wasn't even noon yet, but the sun was already bright. It was going to be hot, that was for sure. I almost envied Rachel heading up to the mountains. It would probably be cooler up there.

"It feels weird to just sit around and relax," I said.

As soon as the words were out of my mouth, I heard a bloodcurdling scream.

"Yaaaaaaahhh!" someone shrieked.

"Oh! Oh! Oh! Oh!" someone else cried.

I sat straight up. Trouble! I could feel the familiar rush of adrenaline. I quickly looked around, checking for the ways to escape, the places where we could stand and fight, the places we might be able to hide for a quick morph. People were running.

No . . . on a closer look, only a couple of girls were running. They were the ones screaming.

"That's Darlene," Cassie said. She sent me a puzzled, worried look.

"Oh! Oh! Oh! Get it away from me!" Darlene screamed. "Get it awaaaaay!"

Darlene ran straight toward us. She ran like the hounds of hell were right behind her. "Help me!" she screamed. "It's after me!"

"What is it?!" I yelled to no one in particular.

"Mice!" this girl named Tracy yelled. "Miiiice!"

Then I spotted them: two tiny, harmless little mice. Two little mice, chasing Darlene like a pair of lions trying to bring down a buffalo.

Darlene dodged right. The mice went right after her. And then something very interesting happened. This guy named Hans yelled, "Darlene! Run this way! I'll stomp them!"

Darlene headed for Hans. Hans raised his foot up, ready to stomp the mice as they shot past. But suddenly the mice turned a sharp left, shot around behind Hans, and tore off after Darlene again.

Right then, I knew. The mice had heard Hans's plan. They had dodged away to safety.

"Real mice don't chase people," Cassie said, giving me a meaningful look.

"No, they don't," I agreed.

"Marco," Cassie whispered. "And he must have dragged Ax into it, too."

"I'll kill him," I said. "Just as soon as we save him."

I raced around the pool. I tore through a mess of overturned chairs and soda cans and paper plates. Cassie went the other way.

"Help me! Help me!" Darlene screamed, running toward the patio door.

"Hey!" Cassie yelled as loudly as she could. "It's just a couple of mice. Nothing to be afraid of."

One of the mice hesitated. Marco had recognized Cassie's voice.

"You know, if those mice want to live, they should go to Cassie," I said, trying to sound like I was making a joke. "Otherwise, someone might *kill* them." Then, under my breath, I added, "Someone like me."

<I heard that,> Marco said to me in thought-speak.

I could hear his thought-speak. But since I was not in a morph, I could not reply. Probably a good thing. I might have used some words I shouldn't use.

It was total pandemonium! Forty kids running around like idiots. Half running away from the mice. Half running after the mice. Everyone making lots of noise.

"Come here, little mice," Cassie said loudly.

We were trying to make Marco realize he had to head for Cassie. I knew he could hear us — mice have excellent hearing.

But Marco either didn't get it, or had decided he wasn't done chasing Darlene.

"Aaaaahhh!" Darlene was not done screaming, either. She reached the patio door. She was still screaming as she disappeared inside her house.

Marco was after her like a shot, with Ax right behind.

<Don't worry,> I heard Marco say in thought-speak a few seconds later. <We're down in the basement. We're demorphing. Just make sure no one comes down to the basement looking for mice.>

"Oh, man," I muttered. I ran for the patio door.

THUMP!

I slammed hard into Hans, and both of us went rolling. No less than eight other people slammed into us, one right after another. It was like some bad football game, all of us jumbled together, yelling and giggling and pushing and trying to untangle our legs and arms.

As it turned out, that pileup saved my life.

I sucked wind and tried to stand up, and the sky above us grew dark.

It was so sudden and so complete that everyone just froze.

I looked up. The sun was hidden behind a swirling cloud of dust. Like a flat tornado. A tornado in a clear sky.

I felt a terrible sensation of dread from deep down inside.

The dust swarm grew solid.

Within seconds, it assumed a shape.

A shape like nothing ever seen on planet Earth.

And then it struck.

CHAPTER 5

Marco

☐kay. *Okay*, maybe it was a little immature to sneak into Darlene's party as a mouse. But you didn't hear what she said about me!

Me and Ax morphed in a vacant lot a block away. Then we toddled on over on our little mouse legs to the party.

Of course, first we had to get used to the mouse morph. See, when you morph you don't just get the animal's body. You get its brain, too. And most animal brains are loaded with different instincts. Usually hunger. Also fear.

The mouse had a lot of each. He was very obsessed about food. And he was one scared little animal. It's often that way when you first morph a new species. As soon as Ax and I achieved total mousehood, those instincts kicked in big time.

RUN! RUN! RUN! RUN!

The mouse didn't like being out in the open, in broad daylight. He was scared of predators. Seriously scared.

RUN! RUN! RUN! RUN!

So we ran. It was like one minute you're a normal human thinking, *Hmmm, isn't it fascinating shrinking down like this, growing a tail, having big whiskers?* And the next minute that mouse brain kicks in and suddenly you are charged up with the energy of a thousand cups of coffee on top of a thousand bowls of Captain Crunch, and you are ENERGIZED!

<I can't control this creature!> Ax wailed. <It's insane!>

<Just go with it,> I said. <It'll chill out eventually.>

Let me tell you: Mice can move on those little legs. It was like being strapped to the front bumper of an Indy 500 car.

ZOOOOM!

We hauled butt, zipping in wild terror over leaves of grass as big as trees, pieces of gravel the size of beach balls, and bugs the size of collies. That much I'm used to. I've morphed small animals before.

But what was sick was that I really, really wanted to stop and eat some of those bugs. There was this one beetle, kind of bluish-black, and the mouse brain was like, *Ah, cool, lunch!*

But it was more terrified than it was hungry, so we just kept running like out-of-control lunatics, and I missed out on the flavor of bug. Eventually, we were able to get some control.

<Ax. You okay, man?> I called to him in thought-speak.

<I am fine. But these mice have very powerful instincts.>

<Yeah. Scared little things, aren't they?>

<Animals develop instincts for a good reason,> Ax said darkly. <If the mouse is cautious, it probably has good reasons.>

<Well, if we see any cats, we'll just morph back,> I said.

<Yes. If we live long enough.>

In any case, we toddled off to the party, two little mice looking for a good time.

Mouse senses are excellent, fortunately. Hearing is great. The sense of smell is great. The eyes are decent, but it's hard to see much when you're only an inch tall and your face is down at dirt level.

Still, I was able to locate Darlene by the sound of her voice. She was talking to her friends about the usual stuff: school, music, some cute guy on TV. Ax and I hid underneath Darlene's chair, so I was able to hear everything pretty well.

All I could see of Darlene was this enormous chair roof over my head — stretched bands of interwoven plastic, bulging down like they might burst and crush me. Quite a distance away I could see her legs, looking like two gigantic pink pillars.

<Well, this is boring,> I said to Ax.

<What did you expect?>

<I expected them to be talking about me, naturally,> I said. Then it occurred to me. I could thought-speak to Darlene! I would just say the word "Marco" in her head. She wouldn't know where it had come from. She'd probably think someone had said it aloud. With thought-speak, you can either do it so everyone hears you, or sort of aim it at just one person.

<Marco,> I said.

"What?" Darlene asked. "What *about* Marco?"

"Nothing about Marco," this girl named Kara said.

"Good, because I don't even want his name mentioned at my party. He's such a jerk. I mean, after what he did? Throwing Baby Ruth bars in my pool? Panicking everybody?"

"He's so immature," a girl named Ellen said.

"No duh," Darlene said. "He thinks he's so cool and so cute, but he's totally *not*. He always makes jokes about stuff that aren't even funny."

Well. I could stand them saying I was immature. That's what girls always say. But saying I wasn't funny?

I would show them funny. Oh, yes.

I took off. I ran for the legs. Ax came after me yelling, <What are we doing?!>

<We're just going to see how good Darlene's sense of humor is,> I yelled back. I ran for that big pink leg. I saw the foot pressing heavily down on the grass. I shot past her heel, which was like a wall to me, and aimed for the toes.

Let me just say this: Darlene thinks she's perfect in every way. But her toenails definitely needed trimming.

I scampered right onto her foot. I zoomed across her foot, then scrabbled wildly around her ankle and back over her toes.

<Yee-HAH!> I crowed to Ax. <That'll give her something else to complain about!>

"Oh! Oh! Ohhhhhhhhh!" Darlene screamed.

Up flew the foot! I jumped off just in time. And then she was outta there, screaming and yammering like a total ninny.

Naturally, I chased her. And naturally, Ax came with me.

It was total, absolute fun! I'm sorry, I know it was wrong and all, but man, it was so cool.

That is, until I heard Hans yelling about how he was going to stomp me. That would never do.

33

I did not intend to be stomped by Hans's big stinky foot.

I heard Jake's big voice yelling. And Cassie's sweeter — but still annoyed — voice.

<Oh, man. It's Jake,> I said to Ax. <Busted.>

I raced for cover, looking for a place to morph back to human. Big stomping feet were landing all around me. They were slow, but man, they were big. Everyone was totally overreacting. I mean, give me a break, I was two inches long! How scary could I possibly be?

Then it occurred to me. The house! We could run inside, race down to the basement where no one would be, morph back real fast, and then . . . Well, and then there I would be, just me and an Andalite. Great. That wouldn't look too strange.

<Ax! Stay with me. We need to demorph. Then you have to do your human morph real quick, okay?>

<I have the feeling, Marco, that this was not a good idea.>

<Nah. Everything according to plan.>

ZOOM! Over the threshold onto the patio! ZOOM! Into the house itself! ZOOM! Past a hysterical Darlene, who was on the couch with a pillow over her head.

ZOOM! Along carpet till we hit linoleum.

Suddenly, the scent of dark places. Mouse places! Yes, it was going to work!

We ran across a step and leapt, falling . . . falling . . . PLOP! to land on the next step. Again and again, step after step, at a speed that felt like we were flying rockets.

It was so cool! If you overlooked the fact that it was maybe slightly stupid.

<Don't worry,> I called to Jake in thought-speak. <We're in the basement. We're going to demorph. Just make sure no one comes down to the basement looking for mice.>

We lost our pursuers. No one followed us down the steps. And even as I ran, I started to demorph.

I was halfway back to human, a strange mix of mouse tail and huge ears and human legs — a scary-looking creature. The way Mickey Mouse would look if he'd been invented by Stephen King. Ax looked even worse, half-mouse, half-Andalite.

Just as I was thinking, *Hey, this will all be fine,* the entire world just flew apart.

Crrrrr-RUNCH!

Sunlight streamed down! The entire roof had been ripped away! The entire roof!

Wood and beams and concrete just shattered and ripped and fell in huge chunks. I couldn't even make sense of it. I mean, the entire world around me was just being shredded. Shredded, like the universe was being run through a food processor.

Then I saw it. It was gigantic! Enormous! A creature that seemed to be made of nothing but teeth and blades and destruction. It was like twenty Hork-Bajir glued together and given dragon wings.

B-R-R-A-A-A-K!

It was ripping the house apart with unbelievable power.

The noise was terrifying. The scream of ripping wood. The shattering crunch of concrete being torn up — just torn up, like it was nothing! Pipes bending. Wires sizzling and popping as they exploded into showers of sparks.

"Look out!" I yelled to Ax with my now-human voice. Beams were falling around us. Splinters were flying through the air.

I barely noticed that I had finished morphing. I was human again. Somehow Ax had kept his concentration and was fully in his human morph.

We were defenseless. Two kids without a weapon between us.

Above our heads, where there had been a house just seconds before, the beast hovered in the sun.

It looked down at us with a dozen weird eyes that seemed to be stuck here and there at random. It stared at us the way I'd seen Tobias stare at his prey.

It was going to destroy us. There was no question in my mind. And no question that it could.

"Oh, man," I moaned. "I don't like this."

Then . . . the eyes all flickered at once. The beast seemed uncertain.

And to my utter relief and utter amazement, the thing began to disperse. He became dust again. Just a cloud of dust that thinned and disappeared.

I was shaking so badly I couldn't stand up. But I was alive.

CHAPTER 6
Rachel

I woke up.

I was on my back, lying on a bed of pine needles and crispy dried leaves. I was staring up at trees. The sun shone through the branches.

My first thought was, *What am I doing here?*

I had no idea how I had gotten to these woods. Or even what woods these were.

"What am I doing here?" I started to say out loud. But the words were garbled, mangled. They were more of a screech than actual words.

I felt a tingle of fear.

What was going on? What was going *on*? Why was I here? Why couldn't I talk?

I shouldn't be here. I should be . . . where?

Where should I be? I tried to concentrate. How had I come here? Where was I *before*? Where . . . where did I belong?

But nothing came. Nothing! I couldn't remember how I'd gotten there. I couldn't remember where I had been. Ever.

Suddenly, it hit me in a wave of dread that made my heart skip several beats: I didn't know who I was. I did not know my own *name*.

I tried to sit up. And that's when I saw.

"Aaaaaaahhhhhhh!" I screamed in a weird, high-pitched shriek.

My legs . . . they were encased in a black leotard. And I could see that the upper half of each leg was shaped like a normal human leg. But the end . . . the bottom half suddenly changed shape. And from the bottom of the leotard, huge talons appeared.

I looked at my hand. Five fingers. Five human fingers, but they sprouted with feathers. There were feathers sticking out of my flesh!

I felt my face. Skin. Skin on my cheeks and my neck. But then, my bristling, feathered fingers felt my mouth.

It was a beak! A hard, tearing beak.

It was a nightmare! That was it, I was having a nightmare! I had to wake up. I had to get out of this dream.

"Aaaaahhhhh!" I screamed again. And the unhuman sound of my own voice frightened me still more.

I had to control the panic. I had to. I had to. But my legs! My face! My hands!

Don't panic, I ordered myself. *You will not panic. You will not panic! This isn't real.*

And yet I could feel the pine needles beneath me. And the warmth of the sun as it lanced through the branches. It all *felt* real.

Was this how I always was? Was I some sort of freak? Half-bird, half-human?

No. I knew that was wrong. And I knew that people did not become birds. And yet here I was, with feathers and a beak, and no memory of who I was. I looked like some horrible creature who was halfway through changing from bird to human — or the other way around.

Was that it? Had I been in the process of changing from one to the other? And which one was I really? Who was I? *What* was I?

Come on, I ordered myself. *Get a grip. Get a grip.*

But I could feel screams boiling up inside me. I could scream and scream and scream.

No. No. Start that and you may never stop, I thought. *Use your head. Think.*

I strained to remember, but it was as if half

my brain were wrapped in a dense fog. I couldn't see through it. No matter how I tried.

You're a human, I told myself silently. *You're human, not a bird. And if you could change this far, maybe you can change more.*

I closed my eyes. I wanted to concentrate, and I did not want to see my body. Terror rattled through me, shaking my bones, churning my insides.

I was human. I wanted to be fully human. Human again.

Then . . . I began to feel changes. I opened my eyes. As I watched, the talons shriveled and split and became toes.

It was revolting to watch. It made me sick. But then I realized something. As soon as I lost concentration, the changes stopped. That had to be it! I must have been changing, and something had broken my concentration. I could not stay the way I was. I was a nightmare. I had to get out!

I felt a shadow over the sun. I thought it was a passing cloud. I couldn't let myself be distracted.

I focused down again. Human. I wanted to be human. I felt the feathers melt into my skin. I felt my beak become soft lips.

The sun was very dim now. Something was blocking it. I felt a chill. I looked up.

Just above the trees, a cloud of dust swirled wildly, like some flattened tornado. It swirled and concentrated.

A dust cloud. But not a dust cloud, really.

As I lay there, I had a terrible feeling. A feeling that this swirling, thickening cloud was watching me. Considering me. Focusing on me.

But I could *not* allow myself to be distracted. I was still not fully human. And I wanted to be human again. Maybe . . . maybe once I was human, I would remember who I was.

CHAPTER 7

Tobias

I have seen a lot of strange things since that first evening when we walked through the construction site where the Andalite prince had landed his damaged fighter.

Back then I was just a kid. A boy. A dork, I guess. It's getting hard to remember. But yeah, I guess I was a dweeb. I remember that I met Jake because he stepped in to save me from some punks who wanted to flush my head in the toilet.

Well, a lot has changed since then.

I've gotten so I can deal with being what I am now. I've accepted the fact that I am no longer completely human. But I'm not completely a hawk, either.

Like I said, I've seen strange things. But

nothing stranger than what I saw that morning as I floated in the high thermals, a mile above Darlene's house.

See, I was flying "cover." It's one of the ways I'm able to help my friends. Marco hadn't *asked* me to fly cover for his idiotic little escapade, but I figured I'd better. Besides, I'd already eaten. A small snake, an unusual delicacy for me. I had nothing else to do, really, but catch a thermal and ride it up.

A thermal is an updraft of warm air. You spread your wings and it lifts you up like an elevator. Once you're up, you can just float there forever. You barely have to flap your wings.

So I was up pretty high. High enough that I could see everything from the edge of the woods to the south, all the way to the center of the city a few miles away. But I stayed low enough that I could still watch Marco and Ax morph.

They ran around like fools till they got a grip on their mouse brains. Then, as they gained control, they set off purposefully toward Darlene's house.

Marco is an extremely smart guy. I don't know if Ax is smart for an Andalite, but he's really smart by human standards. Neither of them really understood how dangerous it is to be a mouse, walking openly across a suburban lawn in broad daylight.

I mean, you might as well just tie raw steaks to your legs and go for a walk with a wolf pack. Hawks kill mice. Cats kill mice. And let me tell you something: Two groups of animals you don't want chasing you are hawks and cats.

From the air I observed one fat tabby cat who spotted them passing by. But I guess he was full, or just feeling too lazy, lying out in the sun. The cat let them pass undisturbed.

I also spotted a Cooper's hawk checking them out. He was definitely thinking about mouse for lunch. I signaled the Cooper's that these were *my* prey and he backed off. Fortunately, I was bigger than he was, and he wasn't hungry enough to fight.

I watched as Marco and Ax reached Darlene's pool party. I relaxed then. If they didn't get stepped on, they'd probably be safe. Still, watching the party made me a little sad. The people seemed to be having a good time. Kids were splashing in the pool and running around and yelling and talking.

It was a whole different universe than the one I lived in. I had the other Animorphs and Ax for friends. But I didn't have friends like myself. Hawks don't get together and have parties. Mostly, when you see another hawk it means trouble, a fight for territory.

Down below, I saw Marco chasing some girl. *Good grief,* I thought. *Why am I not surprised?*

The girl ran inside the house. Marco and Ax ran after her, trailing a posse of guys, one of whom was clearly Jake.

Then I began to see something bizarre. A dust storm. That's what it looked like, anyway. Like one of those little dust devils that kick up out in the desert or prairie.

It swirled like a compact tornado. I was fascinated because wind is very important to me. Wind is life and death to me sometimes.

The tornado was getting tighter. More solid. I strained my hawk eyes to see every detail. I spilled air from my wings and swooped lower to get a better view.

And then . . . it wasn't a dust cloud anymore.

It was a creature! A beast made up of gnashing mouths and whirling blades.

It dived at the house, ripping it apart like it was made out of Legos. It seemed to be chewing its way through brick and wood and shingle. It was like watching a garbage disposal grind up a carrot.

Kids were screaming. They were running wildly, this way and that. Suddenly, half the house was gone. Just *gone*, and I could see straight down into the basement. Straight down at Marco, human once more, and Ax in his human morph.

I folded my wings back and dived like a rocket. Maybe I could distract the beast.

Then, for no apparent reason, the beast began to dissolve.

I pulled up sharply, still a few hundred feet up. I could see Marco practically faint from relief. Ax didn't look too happy, either. But they were both alive. And Jake and Cassie? Both were staring up at the sky in horror.

The dust beast dissolved into a cloud again. A human eye would not have seen anything after that. But I didn't have human eyes. I saw the dust cloud disperse. But I also saw the individual particles streaming away toward the forest.

The particles were moving at incredible speed. They were not being blown by the wind, I was sure of that.

They were moving all on their own. Very fast, toward the woods.

CHAPTER 8

Rachel

Human. Be human!

I focused with all my power on that one thought. I squeezed my eyes shut and tried to remember who I was. What I looked like.

I felt my body change. It was a horrifying sensation. I could hear bones crunching. I could feel a sudden nausea as a human stomach reappeared. I seemed to itch all over as flesh absorbed feathers.

Had I done this before? It didn't seem possible. It was disgusting. Grotesque.

I opened my eyes.

Right above me! What was it?

Mouths with needle-sharp teeth! Staring eyes! Whirling blades!

It was after me!

Should I fly? Should I run? What was I?

I leapt up, hoping I had legs.

Yes! I could run. Yes! I ran. I ran! My own bare feet flashed ahead of me. Human feet. My arms pumped, but they still felt odd. The bones were connected wrong. I ran! Over pine needles that stabbed the tender soles of my feet.

B-R-R-A-A-A-K-K!

It was behind me! It chewed through a tree four feet thick. Chewed it up and left splinters and sawdust behind.

"NO!" I screamed, and my voice was almost human.

NO! NO! It was after me. It wanted to kill me. Why? Why? What had I done? Who was I, that this monster wanted to destroy me?

I raced as fast as I could, but it was faster. Entire trees were ripped from the ground to make way for it. The very ground itself was ripped up as if by some huge plow. The shrieking of destruction was all around me.

What was happening to me?

"Help me!" I screamed. And now my voice was truly human. The last of the changes were occurring. My arms pumped smoothly now. My eyes looked past a normal human nose. The beak was gone.

But the beast . . . the BEAST! It was on me!

Suddenly, a road! Cars flashing by!

I ran for the road. The beast pursued me, ripping a path through the woods.

Cars zooming past! If I ran out into the road, they would hit me. If I stopped, the beast would devour me.

I ran.

SWOOOOM! A car shot past, missing me by inches. Six lanes! A freeway! I ran, hoping against hope to survive.

Horns! Blaring horns!

A truck.

The beast.

It hit the truck, or the truck hit it. I don't know which.

The cabin of the truck was crumpled. I caught a flash of the driver yelling, frantically working the steering wheel.

Then the trailer part, the part that said BEN AND JERRY'S, slammed into the dust beast.

Screeching, screaming wheels! Then, WHAM!

I tripped and went sprawling into the median strip. I rolled down a grassy slope into dirty water. I looked up in time to see the truck turn over and skid wildly down the freeway, spraying sparks.

The beast shredded the trailer. Shredded it! Pints of ice cream exploded around like hand grenades. In the middle of terror I was pelted by pints of Cherry Garcia and Wavy Gravy ice cream.

The beast rose from the truck. The driver climbed up out of the cab and ran.

As the beast rose into the air, a hundred manic eyes looked around. It saw me. There was no doubt about that, it SAW me.

But the eyes seemed confused. They seemed lost. The beast saw me, but did not recognize me.

Suddenly, as I cowered in the ditch of the median strip, the beast simply dissolved into a cloud of dust.

Dissolved and blew away.

Traffic had stopped on all six lanes, as people hung out their windows to witness the spectacle of a tractor-trailer lying across the road.

I climbed shakily out of the ditch. I was trembling so badly I could barely stand. I was muddy and wet and barefoot, wearing a black leotard. I stumbled across the road, toward the sheltering woods.

A man with a camcorder emerged from his car and began taping the wreck. From far off came the wail of a siren.

I just wanted to get away.

Whoever I was.

CHAPTER 9
Cassie

"Tornado my butt," Marco said angrily. "That thing was alive."

We were watching TV in my living room. Jake, Marco, Ax in his human morph, and me, Cassie. It was afternoon. My parents weren't home yet, so we were safe, talking freely.

The news was doing a special report. They had broken into a talk show to show film of what they described as a "freak tornado." They were showing what was left of Darlene's house. The reporter was standing right where we'd had the pool party. You could see Darlene in the background with her parents, picking through the wreckage.

"The storm hit late this morning, just before

noon," the reporter said. "Some young people were having a pool party, and they describe a sort of funnel cloud that appeared quite suddenly out of a clear sky. Some of the kids who were here actually described it as seeming like a monster or a beast. But of course they were quite frightened at the time."

"They were frightened, all right," Marco muttered. "They were wetting their pants. I know."

"The house was virtually destroyed," the reporter went on. "Almost miraculously, there were only some minor injuries. A few of the kids suffered abrasions and minor cuts. The house itself was fully insured."

"That's a good thing," Marco said dryly. "Because we're talking a lot more than a paint job needed there."

"Now let's go out to the freeway where the same tornado — or possibly a second tornado — destroyed a tractor-trailer, holding up traffic for hours."

The screen showed a Ben and Jerry's ice-cream truck that looked like it had been blown apart by a bomb.

Suddenly I saw something familiar.

"Hey! Look!" I said.

"What?" Jake asked.

"It's gone now," I said. "Are we taping this?"

"Yeah," Marco said. "What is it?"

"Back the tape up. Back it up."

Marco reversed the VCR tape. I watched as the camera panned back across the wreck. Then . . .

"Right there! Right there!" I said. "That girl. See? She's only in the shot for a second. Can you freeze-frame her?"

"Why?" Jake asked. "What is it?"

Marco rewound, then advanced the tape a frame at a time. A blurry figure appeared. The frame froze.

"What is the matter?" Ax asked. "Matt-ter? Ter."

Ax can be odd when he's in human morph. Having a mouth and being able to make sounds just fascinates him.

"Look at that girl," I said. "Tall. Blond hair. Barefoot. Wearing a black leotard."

Jake's eyes widened in shocked recognition. So did Marco's.

"Oh, my God," Marco whispered. "It is! It's Rachel. It has to be."

"She must have just come out of a morph," I said. "That's her morphing suit. And being barefoot and all?"

See, when we morph we can't morph much clothing — just something skintight. And shoes? Forget shoes. I've tried morphing shoes. They end up looking like an entire pack of dogs played tug-of-war with them.

"What is Rachel doing out there?" Jake demanded. "She's supposed to be up in the mountains at that camp."

"You know what this means?" Marco demanded. "That thing. That *thing* that came after Ax and me was also right where Rachel was. Coincidence? I don't think so."

Jake shook his head. "No. Not a coincidence." He looked at Ax. "Do you know what this is?"

"No," Ax said. "I do not. It is not any race that I have ever heard of. But I agree: It is no coincidence. Cidence. Co-IN-sid-DENSE."

"Well, what is it?" Marco demanded angrily.

"Tobias told us that it headed toward the forest at a very high speed," I said. "It was heading for Rachel. The timing is right. The location is right. It attacked Marco and Ax, but then it stopped and went tearing off for Rachel."

"Why? What is the point? If it's some Yeerk weapon, it should have finished us off. I mean, it had Ax and me cold."

"We need to talk to Rachel," Jake said. "Cassie?"

"I'll call." I went to the phone, the one in the kitchen. I dialed Rachel's number. I've probably dialed that number every day for years.

On the third ring: "Hello?"

"Hi, Jordan." Jordan is Rachel's younger sister. "Is Rachel home?"

"Duh, Cassie. She's at the gymnastics thing. The camp."

I felt a tingling up my spine. "So . . . so she did go?"

"Sure."

"She didn't come back early or anything?"

"No. Why? Is something the matter?"

"Nah. Nothing. I was just thinking maybe . . . never mind. Later."

I hung up the phone and took several deep breaths. I didn't want to alarm the others. I went back to the living room.

Marco was still yelling at the guy on the TV. "It wasn't a tornado! Are people blind? A tornado does not have teeth."

Jake saw me first. I tried to conceal the fear I felt inside. But I can't hide anything from Jake. He knows me too well.

"What is it?" he asked.

"Rachel. She isn't home. They think she's at the camp."

Jake, Marco, and Ax all just stared for a moment. Then Marco rewound the tape and played it back.

Tall, blond, a model's body, wearing a black leotard and no shoes.

It was Rachel.

And she was definitely not at camp.

CHAPTER 10
Rachel

I spent hours just walking in the woods. Walking and trying to remember.

Who was I?

What was I?

I didn't know. My mind would not answer me.

I remembered how to talk. I remembered what things were called. I knew that the sky was blue, and the moon was white, and the ocean was deep, and that winter was colder than summer.

I knew all the background things of life. It was like watching a TV show where you could see all the sets, but the characters were invisible.

Of me — of who I was and what I was — I knew nothing.

Or not quite nothing. I knew that I was some sort of freak. I knew I could have the feathers and beak and legs of a bird.

And I knew that I had some terrible enemy.

The pine needles and fallen branches made walking painful. But what else could I do? Where was I supposed to go? Some terrible beast was hunting me. Who could I possibly trust?

"Answer me!" I yelled at no one but the trees. "Who am I?"

The sound of my own voice reminded me I had to be careful. The beast from the sky might be out there. Might still be looking for me.

I walked, always hoping the clouds would lift from my memory. I knew I had amnesia. I remembered the word "amnesia." But how had it happened? *That* I could not remember.

I stayed fairly close to the highway that sliced through the forest. I could see flashes of cars through the trees, a few hundred yards off to my right. But I stayed deep enough in the woods that no one from the road could see me.

I could not afford to be seen. Not until I knew what danger I was in.

Then, amidst all the greens and browns of the forest, I saw something bright yellow. It was deeper in the woods. Another few hundred yards deeper.

I crouched down low and walked on bent legs

toward the splash of yellow. I moved as quietly as I could, placing each bare foot carefully.

It was a shack. The yellow was a cotton, ribbed top. From The Limited, probably.

I froze. What? From The Limited? What did that mean? I squeezed my eyes shut and concentrated.

FLASH! A store. It was a store. Clothing. Tables covered with folded tops in bright colors. I was there. I was there shopping with . . . I knew there was someone with me. I could *feel* the fact that someone was with me.

But I couldn't see any more. The memory fragment was only a brief snippet of time. It told me nothing.

I looked again at the shack. It looked like it had been built a long time ago. It was made of logs, some of which were rotted out. Had I been here before? It felt familiar. This place . . . a place like it . . . but no. I was probably just imagining things.

The yellow top was hanging on a clothesline. I duckwalked left to see through the front doorway. It was open. There was no light inside the cabin.

Should I? Could I take the risk?

"If you want to return the item you'll need a receipt," a voice said.

"Yaaahhh!" I yelled, and spun around.

A woman. Old. No, not so old. Just shabby. Wearing so many layers of clothing she looked fat. But she wasn't. She was thin. Dragging a bulging canvas bag.

Not a threat.

I forced myself to calm down. I tried to let the adrenaline flow out of me, but my heart was pounding and my muscles were tensed.

"You'll need a receipt," the woman said again. She stared at me in a challenging way and held out her hand.

"What?" I asked. "Do you know me?"

"If you want to return the item you'll need a receipt," she said again. She said it precisely the way she had the first time. The identical inflection.

She was insane.

"I don't have a receipt," I said.

She looked past me at something. Or nothing. Then she headed for the shack. I don't know why, but I followed her.

She was mentally ill, but she didn't seem dangerous. And I wasn't exactly normal myself.

I don't know what I expected to find inside the shack, but it was a shock: clothing. Piles of it three feet high. In every corner, clothing. Much of it was dirty. Filthy. Some was stained or burned. Some seemed fine.

The madwoman ignored me completely. She

60

opened her dirty canvas bag and began pulling out more items of clothing. Stained shirts. Ripped jeans. One old sneaker.

"Excuse me," I said. "Ma'am?"

"If you want to return the item you'll need a receipt."

"Can you tell me your name?"

She stopped sorting the clothing. She turned a sly grin toward me. "*My* name? Or *its* name? We are two, not one. Yes. Yes. If you want to return the item —"

"*Your* name, please," I said.

"It's gone now," she said craftily. "But it will be back. Oh yes, they'll be back. They never go away forever."

I guess normally I might have been frustrated. I might have even gotten annoyed. But I knew now what it was like to have your brain betray you.

"Who does all this clothing belong to?" I asked.

"MINE!" she shrieked suddenly. "MINE! It's MINE!"

"Okay, okay! Okay. It's yours."

"I found it all. People throw it away. It's mine."

"Yes, it's yours. But I was wondering . . . I don't have any shoes. I thought maybe you could let me borrow a pair of shoes."

"Will that be cash, check, or credit card?"

"I . . . um . . ." I had an idea. Maybe it was

stupid. Maybe it was even a little cruel. I bent down and picked up a chunk of pine bark from the floor. I held it out to the woman. "Credit card."

She took it. She looked at it in confusion. Then she looked up at me. There was something lost and desperate in her eyes. "Is this the store?" she asked.

"It's your store," I said.

She forced a shaky smile. "Let me know if I can help you find anything."

"I will," I said.

I began digging through the nearest pile of clothing. Shoes were stuck here and there. I dug each one out, one by one, and set them in a pile on the floor. I needed a size five. So far I had mostly men's shoes.

"Are you one of *them*?" the woman asked.

"One of what, ma'am?" I replied.

"The others. The ones who live in your head."

"I don't think so," I said. I was focused on my search.

"There's only one way to know for sure," she said in a soft, silky voice.

Success! One size six Reebok, and one size five Converse. They weren't exactly matched, but they were better than being barefoot.

I heard a creak of rusty hinges behind me. I turned to look. The old woman had opened a trapdoor in the floor of the shack.

I started to rise from my crouch, holding the shoes.

WHUMPF!

Something hit me from behind. I tried to suck in a breath, but the blow had emptied my lungs. The woman was all over me, shoving, clawing, scratching, and screaming.

"YEERK! YEERK! YEERK!"

I struggled to fend her off, but she was strong and driven by her insane vision.

I fell. Down through the hole in the floor.

"YEERK! YEERK!" she screamed.

I landed on dirt. I recovered quickly and leaped back up at the opening. The hatch slammed down on me.

I ducked, just in time.

"YEERK! YEERK! YEERK!"

FLASH! A gray, sludgy pool. An underground cavern. Something in the pool, swimming. Many somethings. Seething just beneath the surface of the pool. Like fish. No . . . slugs. Gray slugs.

"YEERK!"

My head swam with the sudden vision. But I couldn't focus on that. I had to get out. I pounded on the splintery wood of the hatch. "Lady, let me out of here! Let me out of here! I don't want to hurt you."

No answer. I looked around. It wasn't a basement. Just a space beneath the shack. Maybe long, long ago it had been some kind of way to escape. Or maybe it was a place to store food for the winter. But it had the feeling of great age.

It was hard-packed dirt on three sides. The fourth side was a wall of vertical logs. I could see through the gaps in the logs. But I did not see a way out.

"Lady, let me out of here. I'm not going to hurt you."

She spoke in a much quieter voice. "No, no. You don't want to hurt me. You just want to crawl inside my head. Like you did before. Crawl inside my head . . . make me . . . make me give you my husband. Make me give him to you. My children. All for you. All for YOU. Controlling me. In my head. But you died, didn't you, Yeerk?"

I felt a terrible coldness. She was insane. *Insane.* And yet . . . why did her raving mean something to me? That word . . . *Yeerk.* It meant something. Something evil.

Was I crazy, too? Was that the truth I was hiding from myself?

CHAPTER 11
Jake

Marco and I took the bus to a place close to where the dust beast had attacked Rachel and destroyed the ice-cream truck.

The bus stopped and we climbed off. We were at a combination gas station and convenience store just off the highway. There was a Denny's across the street and a Dairy Queen not far off.

The wreckage of the Ben and Jerry's truck was at the gas station. It had been towed there to get it off the road. There wasn't much left of the trailer. It had been chewed up and ground into splinters.

"Well," Marco said dryly, "that sure looks like the work of the same creature that ventilated Darlene's house."

"You do realize you shouldn't have been there in the first place," I said. "Someone could have been killed."

"Like I knew some devil beast was going to come after me?" Marco demanded.

I let it go. Marco knew he'd screwed up. At least, I hoped he knew.

"Come on," I said. "You have the bag?"

"Of course I have the bag," Marco grumbled.

We headed for the woods. Once well into the trees we began scanning the tree branches.

<Up here,> Tobias said in thought-speak.

He was on a branch, preening his feathers. He used his beak to sort of comb through each feather.

"Is this really the time to be worrying about your looks?" Marco asked.

<Preening isn't about looks,> Tobias said patiently. <I'm cleaning and straightening feathers. Clean feathers fly better.>

"How do you even get dirty?" Marco wondered. "I mean, flying all the time . . ."

<I was hungry, so I ate a mouse. A mouse just like the one you became this morning,> Tobias said. <It wasn't a very clean kill. Any other questions?>

I smiled as Marco turned slightly green.

"Where's Ax?" I asked.

<He's coming. He's about a mile back. He's fast, but he's on foot, whereas I flew.>

"Did you . . ."

<No,> Tobias answered. <I didn't see anything. No humans walking in this area of the woods at all, as far as I saw. Except for this crazy woman who lives in a shack out here. No Rachel.>

"Okay," I said, "Marco and I are going to morph now. You want to go up top and make sure we're clear?"

Tobias opened his wings and swept low over our heads before catching a headwind and rising up above the treetops.

"Ready, Marco?" I asked.

"Sure. I love this morph. It's cool. This is what morphing should always be like."

We were planning to use our wolf morphs. For one thing, wolves ran in the forest, so we wouldn't be totally out of place. But more importantly, wolves have a magnificent sense of smell.

"Open the bag."

Marco opened the bag and took out a girl's shirt. It belonged to Rachel. She'd left it at Cassie's house. We hoped it would still smell like Rachel. We were going to play bloodhound. We shoved our clothes back into the bag and stood there in our morphing suits — bike shorts and tops. Needless to say, we looked just a bit out of place.

<All clear,> Tobias called down from somewhere above.

"Well, let's do it," I said to Marco.

"You look so Ah-nold when you get that expression," Marco teased.

"So what?"

"So Arnold. Schwarzenegger."

I smiled. "Oh, shut up."

"All ride den, led's do id," Marco said, doing a pretty decent Arnold accent.

I focused on the wolf. We had first acquired the wolf morphs a while back, when we were on a mission to destroy a Yeerk truck ship.

Wolf, I said to myself.

The first change was the fur, gray and shaggy and as rough as carpeting. It sprouted from my human skin in a wave that rippled down from my neck all across my body.

I could see my face bulging out, growing a long snout. It's very odd, because when you're a human you can't really see your own nose. So it's definitely weird to have this long thing sticking out of your face.

Of course, that's not exactly the only weird thing about morphing.

Morphing seems like it should hurt. I mean, there are entire organs inside your body that are changing. Even down to individual cells, everything about you is changed within a couple of minutes.

It doesn't hurt, though. I guess the Andalite scientists who discovered the process made sure of that. If it had hurt, it would have been pain too terrible to live through. Especially when you're doing some really bizarre morph, like into a lobster or an ant, when there's almost nothing left that's even slightly human.

It didn't hurt. But it could definitely creep you out. I could hear my bones shifting and popping and stretching and squeezing. There was a grinding noise when my knee suddenly reversed direction.

"Hey, Jake?" Marco said. He still had most of his human mouth.

I started to answer him. But the sound that came out was more like "Yowwrrllrow."

Marco grinned and at that second his mouth bulged into a snout. His teeth grew and multiplied and became the fearsome weapons of the wolf.

<I don't believe it. It's coming!> Tobias yelled. <It's coming!>

I didn't need to ask what Tobias meant. I looked up at the sky. A dust storm was blowing just above the trees.

<It's coming!>

69

CHAPTER 12

Rachel

"Let me out, you crazy old woman!" I yelled.

I was learning something about myself. I still didn't know my own name, but I knew one thing: Whoever I was, I had a temper.

But the woman was no longer paying attention to me. I could hear her in the cabin above, sorting clothes and muttering to herself.

The anger I felt was good. I realized it kept me from being afraid. There was something about that word . . . "Yeerk" . . . It meant something. Something bad.

FLASH! I was looking through strange eyes. Seeing too well. Seeing not at all. Then . . . a centipede! Bigger than a human, huge! More creatures. Some real, some . . . some that

70

couldn't possibly be real. An elephant . . . a massive, rampaging bear . . . ants that were as big as I was . . . a deadly creature that swung razor-bladed arms and had feet like tyrannosaurs and . . .

FLASH! . . . and a creature dying. Like a horse. No, like a deer. But not a deer. A tail that flashed. Eyes . . . too many eyes. And thoughts! Thoughts that were in my head.

"Get out of my head!" I yelled suddenly.

I gasped. It had been so powerful. My mind had opened and gushed out horrible images. Then it had closed again. Everything was hidden once more beneath a gray blanket.

I smelled smoke.

And the scent was strong. Strong and near. Was the old woman cooking? Making a campfire. Was she . . .

The shack! It was burning!

"Let me out of here!" I cried. "The shack's on fire!"

"You won't get me again, Yeerk!"

"I'm not a Yeerk! Let me out! Let me out!"

The fire spread with stunning swiftness. In less than a minute there were tongues of flame dripping down through the chinks in the floor above me. I could hear it snapping and popping. The smoke poured down in gusts and then blew away, only to come back still stronger.

"Let me out!" I yelled again. But there was no answer.

I was going to burn! I coughed as smoke scorched my throat. I ran to the log uprights that formed the cage. I shoved at them — shoved and pulled, but they didn't move.

I was trapped!

I tried to scream again, but I coughed instead. I could barely breathe. Already my head was feeling light.

Power. I needed power to break out. Power enough to shatter the rotted logs!

I sank to my knees, driven down by the heat. Sparks fell around me, and I brushed them away as they burned my legs and back.

I was too weak. I couldn't do it. But within me . . . something within me . . .

And then it began. I didn't even notice it at first. I was too terrified. I expected the flame-engulfed cabin to crash down on me at any moment.

Suddenly, I began to change.

I was becoming large. So large, so quickly, that my head was rising toward the flames.

Heavy, dark brown fur was growing from my arms and legs.

But what I noticed most was the power. Rippling, massive muscles bulged from my arms and legs and swelled my neck. It was an incredible, giddy rush.

One minute, I was weak and failing and nearing death. The next minute . . . the power! The amazing, straining, bulging, explosive POWER!

CHAPTER 13
Marco

Tobias came shooting down toward us. He wanted to make sure we knew.

<It's coming!>

I was halfway into morph. Could I use thought-speak yet? I decided to try. <We hear you, Tobias. I can see it.>

<Finish morphing,> Jake yelled in my head. <Better to face this thing as wolves.>

I was trembling with fear. I had faced this thing once already that day. I wasn't interested in facing it twice. But Jake was right — better to fight as a wolf than as a human. And this time Jake was with me.

I was on all fours. I could feel the wolf's strength. I could sense the intelligence and in-

74

stincts of the wolf's brain. All the wolf's incredible senses were mine.

But when I looked up to see the beast forming, I knew the wolf wasn't nearly enough. No animal morph could fight this thing!

<Look at it!> I cried.

<Yeah,> Jake said. He was trying to sound brave. But Jake's been my friend for many years. I know when he's scared. He was scared plenty.

<Here it comes!>

The beast of a hundred mouths and a hundred whirling blades came for us. There were treetops in the way. The beast shredded them.

B-R-R-R-A-A-A-A-K!

We ran. It would have been stupid to do anything else. My powerful wolf's jaws were nothing to this beast.

I ran, and I ran fast. Wolves have pretty good speed, and incredible endurance. A wolf can run for hours, all day if necessary. But I didn't think I would get the chance to run that long.

The beast dropped to just a few feet above the ground, leveled off, and came after us. The trees were close together. Too tight for the beast to fit through, so it simply shredded anything in its way.

B-R-R-R-A-A-A-A-K!

The noise was shocking. I ran. I leapt over fallen logs. I dodged around trees. I counted on my rough gray coat to protect me as I ripped straight through thorn bushes.

B-R-R-R-A-A-A-A-K!

The beast ripped a path fifty feet wide through the forest. It was like some nightmare lumberjack. It reduced trees to twigs and splinters in seconds. Wood shrapnel flew everywhere.

<It's gaining!> I said to Jake. <Little by little, it's gaining!>

<The trees. It destroys them, but they slow it down. Just enough.>

<More trees. Thicker trees!> I yelled.

I looked wildly around at a world washed pale by the wolf's poor color vision. There were trees everywhere. Too many! I didn't know which way the forest grew denser and which way it might thin out.

But the wolf knew. The wolf's own instincts led the way. Jake and I both felt it, I guess, because we began turning north.

B-R-R-R-A-A-A-A-K!

The trees grew thicker and there were more of them. The beast chewed its way after us, but it was no longer gaining.

It was not falling behind, either.

<Jake! Marco! What are you doing?> Tobias yelled.

<Heading for denser woods,> Jake said. <Maybe it'll slow this thing down!>

<It is getting thicker up ahead,> Tobias agreed. <But you better hope it wears out soon.>

<Why?> I said.

<Because you have a quarter mile of woods. And then it opens up into a meadow,> Tobias said. <Open grass.>

Jake and I said nothing. We didn't have to. We both knew if the beast didn't tire out before we came out into open country, it would catch us.

And it didn't seem tired.

Just then, as terrified as I was, I smelled something that set off deeper alarm bells in the wolf's mind. Smoke. There was a fire not far away.

And to my acute wolf's ears came the faintest sound of a human voice screaming.

Just as if the beast had heard the same faint cry, I saw the monster shudder. It hesitated.

<Jake! Look!>

The beast wavered and slowed. I could see the meadow through the trees. The meadow where we would surely die.

Except that now the beast was wavering. Suddenly, it turned away.

It turned toward the place that smelled of fire and smoke.

CHAPTER 14
Rachel

"Haaaarrrrgghh!" I cried.

I was in a shower of flames, as bits of wood and fabric fell around me. I couldn't breathe. I couldn't see. But I could hear an insane grinding noise from deep within my own body. And I knew that I was changing.

In all my despair, I could feel the power flowing through me. Awesome power. But was it enough?

I waited as long as I could. I wasn't done changing. But the heat was too great. And the thing that I was becoming hated the fire.

A sudden surge of muscles! A forward rush! I slammed into the half-rotted logs.

Crrr-RUNCH!

The logs broke from the force of my huge body. The logs that had imprisoned me were mere sticks now. I hurtled through them and away from the burning shack.

At that moment, the shack collapsed on itself in an explosion of sparks.

I stood panting. I stood on four legs. I looked down and saw front paws where hands should have been. My paws were covered in coarse brown fur, very shaggy. And I had long, sharp black claws.

FLASH! A bear on its hind legs, roaring and swinging its mighty paws. Creatures all around. Like walking razor blades. They came for the bear . . . came for *me*.

Yes! I thought. *Grizzly bear*. That was it. I had become a bear. Was still *becoming* a bear, because the morphing was not completely done.

"What am I?" I shouted. But the sound that came from my mouth was not human. "Hhhhhu-uuuRORW!"

What kind of creature was I? How could I do this? How could I become a different animal? It was insane. Insane.

Maybe it was that simple. Maybe I was as insane as the woman who had burned down her shack to kill me for being a Yeerk.

Was that it? Was I a Yeerk? What was a Yeerk?

Suddenly, I heard a wild rush of wind. Not

from the burning, crumbling cabin — from above. Up in the air. I looked up, but my human eyes were changing to bear eyes and I couldn't see very well. I only saw a large shadow hovering above me.

A flash of swift movement! It was attacking!

The last of my human body was gone. And now I felt the full force of the grizzly bear's own mind. It was unafraid. And more than that, it was angry.

No one attacked a grizzly. Not if they wanted to live.

I reared up on my hind legs. I must have been ten feet tall. And I knew I was mighty.

"HhhhuuRRRROOOOWWWWRRRR!" I roared. I swung my massive paw at the hovering beast.

But then, a second flash of movement. Another animal, racing swiftly toward us.

<Rachel! Rachel, is that you?> a voice demanded. A voice I did not truly hear, except inside my head.

I looked at the new creature. It had come to a stop, just a dozen feet away. I peered at it with my dim bear vision. It had four legs, like a horse or a deer. But it seemed to have a head and upper body that was almost human. And there was a tail, I was sure of that. The tail was cocked back like a weapon ready to be fired.

For a frozen moment of time, we all three

80

waited: me, the beast in the air, and this new apparition.

<Rachel. Rachel. Is that you in morph? It's me, Ax.>

<Rachel?> I asked silently. <Is that my name?>

And then the beast made of dust attacked.

CHAPTER 15
A x

My name is Aximili-Esgarrouth-Isthill. I am an Andalite. It was my brother, Prince Elfangor, who gave the humans the power to morph. He had been injured trying to drive the Yeerks away from Earth. And, when he crash-landed his fighter, it was Jake, Rachel, Tobias, Cassie, and Marco who found him.

It was Visser Three who killed my brother, so my human friends have told me. Someday I will avenge that death. I must kill Visser Three or be dishonored.

Later, Jake and the others found me. I was the last surviving Andalite from our great Dome ship.

I am not one of the Animorphs. But I fight

alongside them against our common enemy, the Yeerks. And while I am on Earth, I have taken Jake for my prince.

I had gone along with Marco on his foolish venture to the home of the human named Darlene. I knew it was foolish, but I thought it would be better for Marco to have someone with him.

Marco is highly intelligent. But he is also very afflicted by a condition the humans call "sense of humor." I have noticed that Marco's sense of humor sometimes makes him do strange things.

But when the great beast from the sky appeared, I was powerless. Later, the humans asked me for answers. Did I know what this beast was? The humans assume that I must know every terrible thing that lives in this vast galaxy.

But I did not know this creature. And it frightened me.

When we set off to find Rachel, I traveled through the woods. I live in the forest now. It is my new home.

I ran steadily to reach the place where I was to meet up with Tobias, Jake, and Marco.

Then I detected the smoke. I looked up and saw a pillar of smoke rising through the trees.

My eyes swept around me, checking every direction. I must always be very careful not to be seen by humans. One stalk eye followed the pillar of smoke into the sky. And then, I saw not smoke, but dust. Dust that blew faster than any wind.

The beast!

It was coming again.

I ran! Faster than before, with all my speed.

It had to be looking for me. It had come to hunt me down, I was sure of it. Where should I run? Not toward where Jake and Marco were supposed to be. I could not lead the beast to them.

But the fire . . . maybe the smoke would hide me. Yes!

I raced toward the smell of smoke. My hooves flashed, my tail was tucked down tight against my back for speed.

I saw a small clearing. And in the clearing, a pillar of flame. A building of some sort. It was burning rapidly. The heat blasted me. I could hear the noise of dry wood snapping and popping, flames sucking at the air.

But there was a greater noise. The beast! Above me, above the fire, it swirled and roared like a storm.

Then I saw another creature. It was an Earth animal called a grizzly bear. It reared up on its hind legs and bellowed defiance. But that mighty voice was swallowed up in the hurricane howl of the dust beast.

A grizzly bear. Rachel had a grizzly bear morph. I had seen her use it. It had to be her.

<Rachel! Rachel, is that you?>

The huge bear swung its massive head to glare at me. But there was no thought-speak answer.

<Rachel. Rachel. Is that you in morph? It's me, Ax.>

<Rachel? Is that my name?>

Suddenly, the dust beast attacked.

In a rush of hurricane winds, it descended on Rachel. Not on me, but on Rachel! It was her the beast wanted.

She stood firm, unafraid.

<Rachel!> I cried. <Run, you can't fight it!>

The beast of a hundred gnashing mouths descended on the bear. The bear swung a massive paw. It was a blow that would have knocked my head from my shoulders. A blow that would have punched through steel.

The claws raked the dust beast's closest mouth.

"ROOOWWWWRRR!" the bear cried in sudden pain.

Its paw was gone! Simply *gone*. In its place was a shattered, bloody stump.

What could I do? I was desperate. My tail was my only weapon. But the creature would simply grind it off as he'd done with Rachel's paw.

Rachel bellowed in pain from her awful wound, but she struck again. Still standing erect and defiant, she struck again with her other paw.

"HhhhRRROOOOAAAARR!"

This time the entire leg was gone! And now I could see human terror shining through the bear's eyes.

<Rachel!> I cried in despair.

My Andalite tail was useless. I needed something else. Anything! I searched my memory. What morph did I have to fight this monster?

Nothing. Nothing. Rachel's bear was one of the mightiest morphs we had. And she was doomed.

There was nothing left now but to escape.

No! Not to escape. To follow this creature. To find where it hid. To find where it came from.

I had an Earth bird morph. It was called a harrier. It was very fast. I could morph and perhaps be able to follow this monster.

Because one thing was certain: I could not save Rachel.

The dust beast descended on Rachel. It enveloped her completely. I could no longer see her. It was as if a cloud was swallowing her up. The beast shifted and flowed and re-formed to engulf the raging bear that was my human friend, Rachel.

Shaking with fury and horror, I began to morph.

And suddenly, with a speed that was shocking, the dust beast stopped.

It lifted away from Rachel.

It exploded upward, away from her, and came at me! Right at me!

And in the few seconds left to me, I realized . . . *the morphing!* It was the morphing! That's what it was after. It was reacting to the morphing. It was the morphing energy itself that drew the beast.

It lifted from Rachel. I had a flash of her bear body, wrapped in living ropes. The beast had not killed her. It had wrapped her up, as if wrapping a gift.

The living ropes dissolved to rejoin the dust beast and become part of it.

A hundred mouths and a thousand whirling blades descended on me. Now it was after me! And I knew that if I struck it with my tail, it would leave me with a bloody stump.

I could not fight it. To fight was to be shredded.

I stood still. I reversed the morph and regained my complete Andalite form.

I felt the beast around me. It suffocated me. It choked me. It wrapped me tightly in a cocoon till I could not move an inch.

I felt myself being lifted up from the ground. Up and up, faster and faster, unable to see, able only to hear the wild winds of the beast itself.

But now I understood. I knew where it was taking me.

I knew the purpose of the beast.

And with a fear that chilled me to my bones, I realized that I knew its master's name.

CHAPTER 16
Jake

My wolf nose told me a story.

The stench of burning wood was everywhere, but I could still smell blood. Something had sprayed blood over a wide area. A bear. I smelled the powerful scent of a bear.

I sniffed the ground again. Human. Two different humans.

And something else . . . a strange, alien smell. A smell like nothing I could imagine. Until I looked at the tracks: sharp hoof marks. Ax. Ax had been here.

Two humans. One wearing shoes. One barefoot. A bear. Ax. Blood. A fire, still smoldering.

<What do you make of it?> I asked Marco.

<The barefoot person had to be Rachel. So

was the bear. It had to be her. There are no griz-zlies in this forest. And the blood, that's hers, too. Or the bear's, anyway. So she was hurt bad.>

I swallowed anger and fear. I had to stay fo-cused. <What can hurt a grizzly?> I asked, know-ing the answer.

<A man with a gun,> Marco said. <Another grizzly. Or some animal that isn't from Earth. No Earth animal can mess with a grizzly bear.>

<It was that *thing*,> I said.

Tobias swooped down low and slow. <Bear tracks head north. I see tracks, but they're weird. Hind legs only. Like the bear was walking erect. And blood.>

<So Rachel in bear morph tangled with the dust beast,> I said. <She came out of it alive, but she couldn't use her front paws.>

<That's the way it looks,> Tobias said. <The bear tracks stop down by a stream maybe a thou-sand yards from here. After that, I don't see any-thing. She must have morphed back to human.>

<Which way did she go?> Marco asked. <Up-stream? Downstream?>

Tobias came to rest on a branch. <I don't know. I looked. I didn't see her. I should have gotten here sooner. I should have known when it let you two go that it was going off after her.>

<Tobias, no one understands this monster. You couldn't have known what it would do. None

of us could,> I said. It sounded reasonable. But in my mind I was thinking that I should have known. I should have guessed.

<What's Ax's story in all this?> I asked. Blaming myself was not the point right now. <Ax was coming to meet us. He sees the fire, goes to investigate it. Maybe then he sees Rachel? Or Rachel in bear morph? Were they both here at the same time?>

<I don't know,> Marco said. <Maybe. Lots of Andalite tracks all together here. Then, look — they just stop. Right here. No Andalite scent past this point. It's like he was just lifted up and carried away.>

Tobias said, <So he gets here, sees Rachel and the beast going at it. Ax is a brave guy. He jumps into it. Rachel gets away. She's bloody, but she gets away. And Ax? Why isn't he still here? Or else why don't we see a separate set of Andalite tracks leaving? Or at least see his body?>

No one said anything. We all feared the worst. I was remembering what the beast had done to Darlene's house. And to the trees. Maybe it didn't leave bodies behind. Maybe there was no body left after it was done.

<Andalites are tougher than they look,> Tobias said. <I'm with Ax a lot, out here in the forest. Don't write him off.>

<Yeah,> I agreed, trying to sound hopeful. <We've been in morph a long time. We need to use what time we have left to get to civilization and morph back. I have to at least check in with my folks or they'll have cops out looking for me.>

<We can't just stop looking,> Marco said. <Tobias only has an hour of good light left. After that, there won't be anyone trying to find Rachel. Or Ax.>

<I'll use that hour,> Tobias said. He opened his wings and flapped wearily back up into the sky.

<We'll come back tonight,> I told Marco. <Have dinner with your dad. Then we hook up at Cassie's barn.>

<Jake, what is going on?> Marco asked me as we trotted swiftly back toward the road. <Is this the Yeerks?>

<Who else could it be?> I asked.

<But look, if it's them, then they know who we are. I mean, this thing came right after me and Ax. It went after Rachel. It went after me and you. It *knows* who we are. So why don't the Yeerks just move in on us? Why not show up at our homes?>

<That's the question,> I agreed. We had reached the road. The bus would come by soon. It was time to demorph. <That is exactly the question we need to answer.>

<Yeah, that and the question of where Rachel is, and why she doesn't go home.>

<And one more question,> I added, as I felt my human body emerge from within the wolf. <How do we stay alive?>

**Don't miss out on the rest
of the exciting story
coming soon in PART II of
The Andalite's Gift!**

Don't miss

ANIMORPHS™

#8 The Alien

I morphed as quickly as I could, while being careful not to fall over as my third and fourth legs disappeared. At last, I stood on just two legs. It's both frightening and exciting. I mean, there you are, tottering back and forth with nothing to hold you up. Your feet can't grip, and they are too short to be much help in balancing.

All you can do if you start to fall is stand on one leg while you throw the second leg out to catch yourself. It's very unreliable. I don't know why humans evolved this way. They are the only species on this planet to walk around on just two legs, without wings or a tail to hold them up.

And I've certainly never heard of any other intelligent species trying to walk this way.

"Hey, grab him," Jake yelled as I began to lean back.

"Got him," Cassie said. She helped support me as I finished the morph.

Last of all the mouth appeared, a horizontal split in my face.

"Are you done?" Jake asked me.

"Yes. I am fully human." The sound delighted me. It's an amazing talent, this ability to make complex sounds. "Human. Mun. Hyew-mun. Human. Huh-yew-mun."

"Um, Ax? Don't do that, okay?" Jake said.

"What? What-tuh?"

"That. Where you play with every sound like it's a new toy."

"Yes, my prince. Not a toy. Toy! Toytoytoytoy . . . . Sorry."

"This should be interesting," Cassie said, looking at Prince Jake.

Tobias came swooping low and rested on a tree branch. <It's kind of sweet,> he said. <Ax's first day of school.>

"His *only* day of school," Prince Jake said quickly. "This is just so he can learn how to be a more believable human. One time."

Prince Jake held up a single finger, indicating the number one.

"Yes, that is one," I agreed. "Now, let's go to school. I am looking forward to it. To it. Tewit."

"Remember, you're my cousin Phillip, from out of state."

"Phillip," I repeated confidently. "Phillip. Lip. Philup. Pah."

I like the sound the human letter "p" makes.

I set off toward the squat building that was the schoolhouse.

<Have fun,> Tobias said. He sounded just a little wistful in my mind. It was a strange thing, I guess. I, an alien, could go to his school. But he could not.

"I will," I called back over my shoulder.

Unfortunately, bending that way made me fall over. It takes practice to walk on just two legs.

COMING IN JUNE

*He's a cross between a deer, a scorpion, and a human.
But is this Andalite prepared to fight?*

"Are you done?" Prince Jake asked me.

I considered. I was standing precariously on two legs. I possessed two strong arms and ten strong fingers. I was mostly without fur. My eyes were weak and totally unable to see anything except what was in front of me. My hearing was good. My mind was functioning normally.

And I had a mouth. "Yes," I said, using my mouth. "Yessss. Sssss. Yes-suh. I am in human morph."

I had morphed into a human.

ANIMORPHS #8:
THE ALIEN

K.A. Applegate

COVER SHOWS
AN ALIEN
MORPH!

Visit the Web Site at: http://Scholastic.com/animorphs

WHAT DO YOU THINK?

Hey you guys! We want to hear what you think about Animorphs. Just answer the questions below, fill in your name and address on the back of this sheet, and send your survey back to us: **Animorphs Survey Scholastic Inc. 555 Broadway, New York, NY 10012-3999**. Thanks!

1) How did you first find out about Animorphs?

- [ ] School Book Club
- [ ] Local Bookstore
- [ ] friend/family
- [ ] Library
- [ ] School Book Fair
- [ ] Web
- [ ] TV commercial
- [ ] other_____

2) Who is your favorite character?

- [x] Jake
- [ ] Cassie
- [ ] Rachel
- [ ] Marco
- [ ] Tobias
- [ ] Ax

3) Which of these characters do you like reading about most?

- [ ] Hork-Bajir
- [ ] Taxxons
- [ ] other_____
- [x] Yeerks
- [ ] Visser Three

4) Which is your favorite book?

- [x] #1: The Invasion
- [ ] #2: The Visitor
- [ ] #3: The Encounter
- [ ] #4: The Message
- [ ] #5: The Predator
- [ ] #6: The Capture
- [ ] #7: The Stranger

5) Which of these magazines do you like to read?

- [ ] Nickelodeon Magazine
- [ ] SI for Kids
- [ ] Highlights
- [ ] Boys Life
- [ ] Other_____
- [ ] Girl
- [ ] Teen Beat
- [ ] YM
- [ ] Sassy

6) Which of these book series do you read?

- [ ] Goosebumps
- [ ] Baby-sitters Club
- [x] Fear Street
- [ ] Sweet Valley Twins
- [ ] other_____

7) Where did you get your most recent Animorphs book?

- [ ] School Book Club order
- [x] Bookstore
- [ ] School Library
- [ ] Public Library
- [ ] School Book Fair
- [ ] Supermarket
- [ ] other_____

8) How do you buy your Animorphs books?

- [ ] In numerical order
- [ ] Only the most recent titles
- [x] Based on the cover design

9) Do you know about the Animorphs web site at http://www.scholastic.com/animorphs?

- [x] Yes
- [ ] No

10) If so, how often do you visit the Animorphs web site?

- [ ] Never
- [ ] Once a month
- [ ] Several times a week
- [ ] I hardly ever visit it
- [ ] Once a week
- [x] Almost everyday

11) How many Animorphs books have you read? _8_

ANIMORPHS™

Now tell us about yourself!

☐ Boy ☐ Girl

Name _____ Birthdate _____
                                          Mo./ Day/ Year

Address _____

City _____ Zip _____

State _____

Telephone (_____) _____ Grade _____

JOIN US
ANIMORPHS™